IMAGINE THAT

Licensed exclusively to Imagine That Publishing Ltd
Tide Mill Way, Woodbridge, Suffolk, IP12 1AP, UK
www.imaginethat.com
Copyright © 2021 Imagine That Group Ltd
All rights reserved
2 4 6 8 9 7 5 3 1
Manufactured in China

Written by Georgina Wren
Illustrated by Gabi Murphy

ISBN 978-1-80105-006-7

A catalogue record for this book is available from the British Library

Mummy Loves Me

Written by
Georgina Wren

Illustrated by
Gabi Murphy

My mummy says she loves me,
she says it every day,

But she doesn't have to say it, I know it anyway.

I wake up very early and
I stretch and I yawn.

She's always right here with a hug that's nice and warm.

When I'm ready for my breakfast
there's a rumbling in my tummy.

Mummy makes it for me and
it's always really yummy.

When we get dressed together,
Mummy lets me choose my clothes.

She pulls my top over my head,
and my socks over my toes.

If I'm playing in the garden,
and I fall and hurt my knee,

Mummy makes it better with a special kiss for me.

At the swimming pool I jump
in like a flash!

Mummy smiles and laughs
as I splosh and I splash.

Now I can use the potty, nearly all alone!
Mummy's there to help me, but I use it on my own!

We like to draw together and
I use my favourite colours.

Mummy puts my picture on the wall with all my others!

Whenever I need a cuddle,
in the day or in the night,

Mummy's always there –
she makes everything all right.

Just before I fall asleep, my mummy reads to me.

We snuggle up together – just Mummy, books and me!

I know my mummy loves me,
I told you I can tell.

She really, really loves me ...

... and I love her so much as well.